HUBBLE BUBBLE GRANNY TROUBLE

For all those grannies who are wonderfully different!
T.C.

For Granny Sue, who wears funny hats, and Granny Clare,
who cooks a mean froggy-poop soup.
J.B.

First published 2011 by Nosy Crow Ltd
The Crow's Nest, 10a Lant Street
London SE1 1QR
www.nosycrow.com

ISBN 978 0 85763 027 8 (HB)
ISBN 978 0 85763 028 5 (PB)

Nosy Crow and associated logos are trademark
and or registered trademarks of Nosy Crow Ltd.

Text copyright © Tracey Corderoy 2011
Illustrations copyright © Joe Berger 2011

The right of Tracey Corderoy to be identified as the author
and Joe Berger to be identified as the illustrator of this work has been asserted.

A CIP catalogue record for this book is available from the British Library.

Printed in China

3 5 7 9 10 8 6 4 2

HUBBLE BUBBLE GRANNY TROUBLE

Tracey Corderoy

illustrated by

Joe Berger

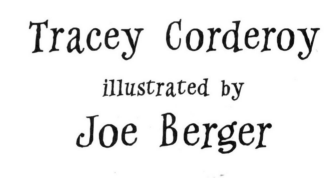

nosy crow

. . . She wears such funny hats.

She's got a huge menagerie

of cats and frogs and bats!

She takes them to the cinema.

They take her to the zoo.

But – somehow – everywhere they go,

they never need to queue!

NOW SHOWING

SCARY POPPINS

BURP!

My granny's kind of different. She cooks this icky soup.
I swear she uses slime and sludge and bits of froggy-poop!

I beg her for fish fingers, but Granny shakes her head . . .

"Oh, yuck!" she cries. "How horrible!
Here – have some gloop instead!"

My granny's kind of different. Her friends are different too.
They just don't do the kind of things
that **OTHER** grannies do!

They make things disappear. My friends all think it's cool . . .

. . . but Granny really went too far that day she helped at school!

My granny's kind of different. She drives a crazy car.
It's got no roof or seats or wheels
– it's really most bizarre!

When we're in a traffic jam, she makes her car-thing fly.
"Hey, Granny – mind that aeroplane!
Oh, please slow down!" I cry.

My granny's kind of different. So one day, "Hey," I said,
"how about we make you kind of 'normalish' instead?"

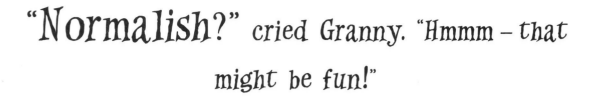

"Normalish?" cried Granny. "Hmmm – that
might be fun!"

We started off by knitting hats, though Granny

just did

one!

Later on, we caught the bus
and tootled into town.
"See . . ." I said. "No aeroplanes!
No flying
upside down!"

We visited the pet shop
to choose a 'normal' pet . . .
No fangs, no warts, no burps,
no smells – as nice as you could get!

Then Granny got her hair done. It looked so very smart.
Combed and curled and neatly twirled . . .
a proper work of art!

Now Granny looked so normal, but something wasn't right.
She seemed like someone else's granny,
strolling home that night . . .

Next day, I went to see her
but Granny was in bed.

"Oh, dear!" I cried.
"Whatever's wrong?"
"I'm kind of . . . bored!" she said.

So down the stairs I led her
to cook some gloopy soup.
(I added extra slime and sludge and even froggy-poop!)

Then we sat together. "What shall we do?" I said.
"You were nice and different,
but now you're sad instead."

"Not for long!" cried Granny, shaking out her bun.
"All my friends are due at two to have some granny fun!"

So Granny got things ready,
while I let in the bats.
Then poked around the flowerpots
to find the frogs and cats.

My granny's kind of different. That's how she's meant to be.
I love my granny JUST like that and know that
she loves me!

She's taking me on holiday.
We won't need woolly hats . . .

just swimsuits . . .

. . . sixteen cats and frogs

and thirty batty bats!

BURP!

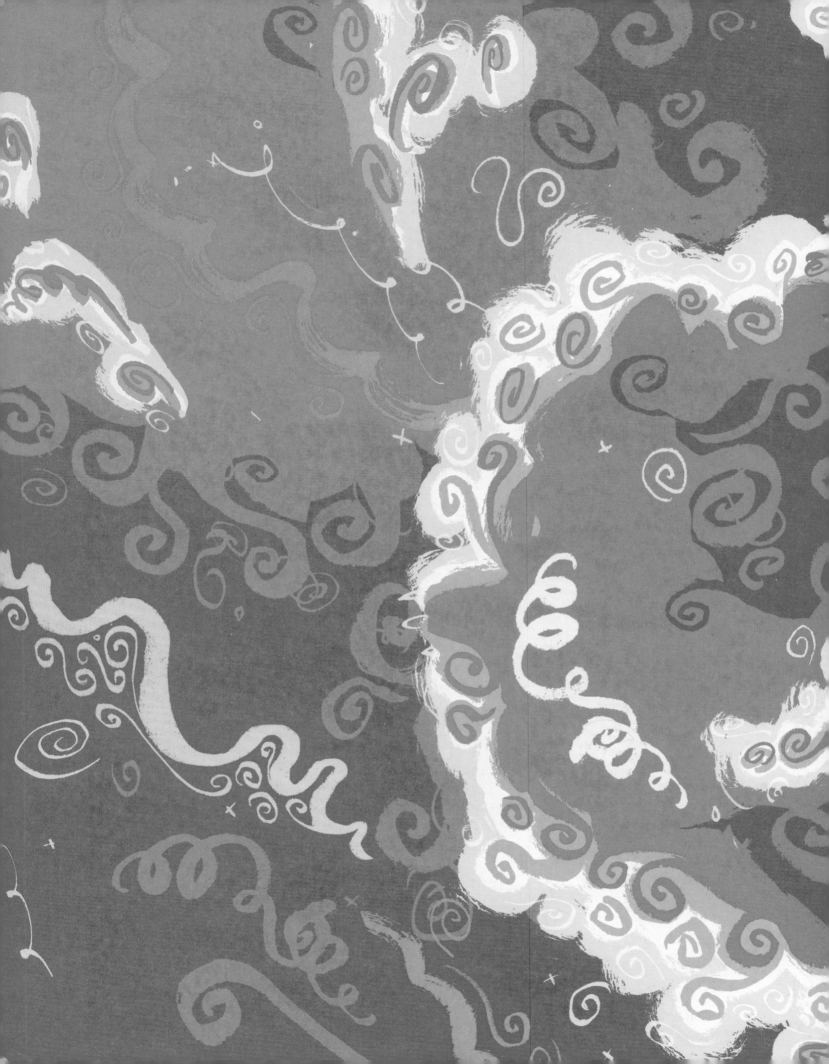